I0633451

In the Photic Zone

essays by

Joanne Jacobson

Finishing Line Press
Georgetown, Kentucky

In the Photic Zone

ACKNOWLEDGMENTS

Essays from this chapbook have appeared in the following publications:

"The Sight of Blood," *Hektoen International: A Journal of Medical Humanities*
"The Brain Has Its Secrets," *The Ilanot Review*
"Garden Hunter," *Fourth Genre*
"For Richard (Every Love Its Own World)," *Sonora Review*

Publisher: Leah Huete de Maines
Editor: Christen Kincaid
Cover Art: Ellen Wertheim
Author Photo: Ellen Wertheim
Cover Design: Elizabeth Maines McCleavy

Order online: www.finishinglinepress.com
also available on amazon.com

Author inquiries and mail orders:
Finishing Line Press
PO Box 1626
Georgetown, Kentucky 40324
USA

Contents

for Tahl, Ali, Rahz, and Ziv

"The photic zone, also referred to as the euphotic zone, is defined as the layer of water that receives sufficient sunlight to allow for photosynthesis to occur."
—*The Environmental Literacy Council*

1. THE WORLD TURNED INSIDE OUT

Deep into rural Illinois the world has been turned inside out, the aftermath of more than twenty-five years of strip mining: blasting, drilling, hauling to the surface deposits of coal buried three hundred million years ago. My grandfather used to bring our family to this place, where the company he worked for owned mines. By then the giant machines that had scooped out soil and rock were long gone, and the raw pits they slashed into the earth had filled in with water. The ugly wounds had turned into lakes surrounded by new-growth trees and stocked with bass and bluegills and bullheads that we fished for. Docks and ramps had been built for swimming and boating—and for forgetting what had been here before, what had been done to the land.

But a harvest of memory had been left as well. Long before coal, lush forests of ferns and mosses emerged across this midsection of the continent out of a retreating prehistoric soup of mosses and shallow seas. Coal would take shape from the remains of life, from the soft, porous peat created by decaying vegetation and then compressed over millions of years. My father and I would head out each morning to search for ferns that had been lifted to the surface by mining, preserved in stone exactly as they had grown, delicate as ever. We'd hold each one in the palm of our hands, the rock warmed by the summer sun, and admire the ancient life that it revealed. And we'd trace the tiny veins that fed the still-translucent leaves from the thicker stems, the difference between them palpable beneath our gently exploring fingertips.

When we returned to our motel with a shoebox full of fossils, we'd find my little sister playing in the shallow end of the pool. On a table next to a chaise lounge, my grandfather, wearing a sleeveless white undershirt tucked into his suspendered pants, would already have deposited a bottle of Scotch. My grandmother would have laid out the lunch that she'd packed the night before: corned beef layered in wax paper, sliced loaves of rye bread and bottles of seltzer; paper plates and cups and napkins. There would be pickled tongue as well, stacked in thick oval slices: fleshy relics of a once living body.

As a teenager I often skipped school with a friend and took the commuter train to the Chicago Loop, where my grandfather worked into his eighties in the nearly new Prudential Building—at forty-two stories the second tallest building in the city. We'd ride one of the elevators, the fastest then in the world, to my grandfather's office, where he would ceremoniously hand each of us a pass to the building's observation deck, reached by the world's highest escalators. Struggling against the winds that strafed the high deck, we could see blocks of buildings unspooling into the distance along the water.

Chicago's rise began with the miracle of location, with the web it drew in every direction over the turning surface of the earth, converting raw nature—forests, animals, plants—into production, and dispatching product to market. The 1955 Prudential Building—*The Rock!*—made a silver pivot at the city's heart, where railroads had since the mid-nineteenth century moved everything. Of all this my friend and I knew little. But from the Prudential Company's still new building we could look down over the Illinois Central tracks laid down in the age of making things, and see the gray and dirty layers of a past that had already been superseded by money made invisibly in finance and real estate and insurance.

*   *   *

In his garden my father took care among the lilies of the valley not to crush the delicate white blooms with his heavy cordovans. He stroked the peony blossoms that rose nearly to his shoulders, a miracle of balance teetering above the earth. And he called out with delight when he uncovered a cow's molar near the backyard mulch pile, explaining to me from his knees how the land on which we were making our lives now was once, just in the last century, a farm.

My father had contempt for encyclopedias and the pre-digested information that they doled out, he believed, to lazy readers. So I held in secret the summer days I spent in the neighborhood branch of the public library cradling the heavy volumes in both my hands, settling them in my lap, letting the worn covers fall open to random spots where the world felt preciously revealed to me: Boer Wars, lemongrass, Mauritius, paramecia.

My father kept his own secrets, dreams that he never spoke of but that were clearly driving him hard. He spent weekends by himself on the roof of the three-story, hundred-year-old red brick house that my parents bought when my father joined his first medical practice, sealing his great suburban claim from the damaging work of the seasons: spring's chill rains, summer's beating sun, autumn's winds, and winter's relentless midwestern cold and ice. From up there my father could see houses like ours standing in rows, big steady things slotted between rectangles of living green grass and fixed in a grid of sidewalks and streets. He never spoke of the hopes that must have shaped that weekend labor, of ownership, property and status; of postwar eagerness to strip away and then to start from scratch with tools and hands; of committing to history what used to be prairie—as though this ground could be forever remade, and he the one to remake it.

Yet everything he worked at during those years—the house, his marriage; his medical career, which steadily foundered at a time when doctors were acquiring unprecedented wealth—was steadily undone by anger and doubt that lurked, without words, beneath the surface. He remained an unpredictable presence in our household, set off suddenly at dinner by the mention of a colleague or a family member who he felt had passed him over for a collaboration or an invitation; driving drunk, silently picking up speed instead of slowing down as traffic lights turned yellow. And the rough voice in which he answered my mother's call to come in from the garden for lunch had animal in it—sending me pounding up the wooden back stairs, slamming the screen door behind me as my mother had told me a million times not to do.

Then there my father would be on a sleepy Sunday afternoon, slipping a classical LP out from its cardboard jacket, taking care not to tear the delicate paper inner sleeve, steadying the vinyl 33 rpm disk with one hand as he eyeballed the distance to the slowly spinning turntable. He'd let the diamond needle drop so softly, hitting the exact mark without a sound, releasing into our living room a full string section, nearly two-thirds of a concert orchestra, lush as a garden in full spring. Whose gentleness was that?

*   *   *

On one of our summer trips to the old mining grounds, not long after my parents divorced, my father brought along his new girlfriend, a young secretary hardly ten years my senior. When we finished loading his car in Chicago, he pointed with pride to the brass plaque Sharon had inscribed and installed on the dashboard over the glove compartment: *Handsome Devil*. He still lacked the nerve, I think now, to draw his parents and his daughters into the raw circle of sexuality, and he shared a motel room on that trip with my sister and me rather than with Sharon. I would hear much later that Sharon had tried to kill herself after my father broke up with her. But on that weekend he brought us uncomfortably close to the force that crackled between them at that unanticipated transition in his life.

At the end of our vacation day, the six of us jammed back into the car and headed toward the small nearby city where my grandfather insistently remembered a restaurant from the time, more than thirty years before, when his company was still running the mines. As we slowly searched, my grandfather released from the back seat a loud sneeze, and then reached into my grandmother's lumpy bag for a tissue—managing instead to cut himself on an exposed razor blade that she had, astonishingly, left buried inside. In a minute my grandfather had flipped the lock below the window at his side, swung his long body out the door, and slammed it behind him. He bent to my father's opened window, announced that he was going to find a bandage, and headed off, one hand clenched over the bleeding other, without looking back. Behind the wheel, my father remained stilled by unarticulated rage while my grandfather walked into the distance, a lone figure backlit against the late afternoon summer sun as though in a movie.

Time seemed to freeze inside the car around our silent

group. I could feel myself filling with hot desire to escape from these people bound, it seemed, to one another and to me by airless, choking uncertainty. No adult turned with words toward either of the two wondering children. Nor did anyone move or speak as my father started the engine again to prowl the unfamiliar streets until we found my grandfather and pulled him back among us.

*   *   *

Today the Mazonia-Braidwood State Fish and Wildlife Area website tells me that the earth there is no longer littered with what my father and I could simply bend to our knees and find. Visitors now must collect rock "concretions" from the rubble, must use a hammer, wear protective eye gear, carefully tap and split the rocks—and be prepared to be left holding a hunk of blank stone: "Not all concretions contain specimens!" Of the presence of humans here only place names remain, reminders of ancient Native settlements and of the seventeenth-century French explorers who arrogantly followed, penetrating hundreds of miles into the interior of the continent: Mississippi, Peoria, Chicago, Marquette; *Joliet*, where we left my grandfather wounded in the street.

That scene in my father's car remains for me a living tableau of family secrets like the ones fixed nearly two thousand years earlier by molten rock at Pompeii. Who knows what the members of those doomed families were to one another, what tendernesses those Roman fathers and mothers shared as volcano-hot ash began to fall around them in the streets and into the loggia of their houses, or during the quotidian times before they were faced with the sudden imperative of survival?

In medicine, what cannot be seen from the surface is termed "occult." My father's cardiac bypass surgery half a century after he and I collected fossil ferns together would take place far from my knowing. I'll never unlock why he waited weeks to call me with news of his recovery, skipping over the story of his blocked heart and hospitalization, making it impossible for me to help him—leaving those witches poised as ever to hurt, to strike out of hiding and to do so many kinds of damage.

What feelings did my father and my father's father hide, silently, close? I could hear my grandfather murmuring into my hair in Yiddish before I left his Prudential Building office near to the Chicago sky, "my *shaineh maideleh*," his beautiful girl. But I want more than memory: I want to empty the world of its secrets. At the heart of the continent lies my heart, and these people, buried now with their mysteries.

2. THE SIGHT OF BLOOD

None of us live to adulthood without seeing our own blood; growing up, I witnessed my blood flow free of my body too many times to count. The bleeding knee picked clean of leaves and gravel after my father sent me spinning down the driveway on my birthday bike; the splinter's wake of red, thin enough to be erased with a single swipe of my hand. The embarrassing mark of puberty on school clothes. The fall that sent me in search of help, bearing into the back seat of a taxi the unseemly memory of myself spilled onto cement, my chin gashed and bloody. The accidents that befall most human beings making their clumsy, not always attention-paying, way through the world, trailing the memory of blood spilled—freshly moist, then scabbed in the air and light. The body's fragile spots opened and then quietly closed.

But the year I turned sixty, blood's invisible pathways to my brain became mysteriously blocked, shaking my world, sending out muddled danger signals: a saw-toothed rainbow that drifted over my vision with greater and greater frequency; words that stuck to one another in my mouth. In the emergency room I learned that blood can slowly transform the self in secret and make a person different in a second. Suddenly I was a patient with a frightening diagnosis, a rare clotting disorder that only a hospital would enable me to survive.

Thrombotic thrombocytopenic purpura affects just a handful of people in a million. The treatment of choice is plasmapheresis: a procedure in which the patient's entire blood supply is siphoned off and centrifuged so that the plasma containing rogue antibodies and damaged enzyme can be replaced with healthy donor plasma. I have lived now to see my blood intentionally emptied. Tethered by the jugular to a big machine, I have witnessed one set of tubes fill with my lifeblood while another, mixed with clear donor plasma, sends blood circling back. And even as blood has been reiterated to me as a physical thing, a fluid like any other washing in and out of my body, it has been revealed in the slowly passing hours of plasma exchange as a force—pulsing deep as my heart.

*   *   *

Blood has long been endowed with mysterious power, subject in virtually every culture to regulation. In the biblical Temple where holy men in white came alone into God's presence, the magic of expiating guilt and of reaching the divine with thanks depended on draining entirely of blood the sheep and the goats whose corpses were laid out upon the sacrificial altar. Holding a living pigeon or a turtledove between the palms of his hands, the priest would pinch off the bird's head and rip open the body by the wings, letting its blood empty over the altar before offering the bird to the fire.

In its prohibition against eating or drinking blood, *Leviticus* set for members of a precarious desert tribe the most radical of boundaries: the threat of abandonment to the wilderness. *Anyone who partakes of it shall be cut off.* Centuries later, my great-grandfather became the ritual butcher in turn-of-the-twentieth-century Michigan, tasked with slaughtering kosher meat for the tiny group of Jews who had settled there after leaving Eastern Europe. To him fell the responsibility of administering death in the bloodless way of tradition, so that members of the community could eat what he killed.

The seventeenth-century physicians who first experimented with blood transfusion permitted themselves to carve the living flesh of dogs and horses and deer so that they could observe hearts beating, the red and the blue of circulation. Still, when scientists began transfusing animals, they recognized blood as a medium charged with essential spirit. They selected for transfusion animals whose dispositions they saw as desirable and hoped to pass on to humans: lambs and calves, for example, for their gentleness.

What animal, I wonder, would I allow access to my own veins? What beast would I ask to give its life for me, to be stitched to me; to be my intimate, my bleeding ally? Alien as those brute scenes of sacrifice and early transfusion may now feel, they speak for human beings' recognition that blood is a fundamental element of what we share with other living things. We remain who we were then, as much *body* as we were in the world that gathered in robes around desert wells for the water upon which human life depended; *animal* among the species saved by Noah two by two.

*   *   *

Blood has taken me to the boundary between life and death, between modern science and ancient spirit. The heavy tubing taped to my head was unwound every day in the hospital, and I was left lashed to the lumbering machine—watching what used to be invisible to me, observing what used to be whole disassembled before my wondering eyes.

How could I not be changed by this, by the sight of my own blood?

Have I already been transformed by the plasma from human donors that's been mixed like syrup into my blood, saving me but invisibly changing me—if not to a lamb or a calf or a dog, then perhaps to someone who will die young from a rare disease?

In the hospital I waited in bed for results from dawn blood draws, so unobtrusive that they barely interrupted my sleep: for my "numbers," my daily platelet count. A bit of red always seeped into the clear plastic tubing splayed across the back of my hand, the quickly accessible beachhead established at every patient's hospital admission in case of an emergency. I hoped each day for information that would mark my progress toward recovery, my movement back into the self that used to be *me*. But that self, the self that hardly gave thought to blood, had retreated forever, transformed by invisible drama.

Blood is in so many ways ordinary; the tactile, visible stuff of human life. It was transported during the London Blitz in modified milk bottles packed into milk crates, delivered to the bleeding wounded throughout the wrecked city by converted ice cream vans. And yet we recognize in what makes blood as mundane as daily, pumping life what makes violently spilled blood so shocking, and such a familiar metaphor for loss of life.

To this day, the blood lost by communal martyrs remains a sacred responsibility of the Jewish community. It is scraped from the ground by volunteers and buried with the dead, returned to the earth with what is left of bodies clad in the clothes they were wearing when they were murdered. No martyr, I searched for days at the spot in front of the apartment building where I had tripped on an untied shoelace. On my knees I looked for a rust-colored stain on the soiled city sidewalk, wondered if a neighborhood dog might have lapped up my blood as I left for the ER with a paper towel pressed to my chin.

3. THE BRAIN HAS ITS SECRETS

Alone in bed I perform some quiet reconnaissance. I can feel flesh, ridged like a walnut, fitted neatly inside the shell of my skull. The signal of my blood is starting to come in like a radio, pulsing at the frequency of life I already know. Still the soft huddle in my brain hangs suspended, remote and uncertain as a distant, blinking star.

In the waiting room I survey other patients completing their clipboarded forms. They leaf restlessly though *The Wall Street Journal*, through *People* stories about unexpected celebrity breakups and the murder trial of Michael Jackson's doctor. All of them must have their secrets as well. The man slouching in an Armani suit tapping the arm of his chair with car keys, marking the time that he seems certain he's wasting here. The couple holding hands, intent upon a morning TV news story as though they hope it will never end—without leaving a clue as to which of them is the patient. When my name is called, I'm escorted by a technician in medical white and pointed behind a canvas curtain. I unhook my bra and take off my wedding ring and my watch, the metal items that might confuse the machine's magnetic forces. I let my head be taped to the gurney, let plastic flippers close over each of my arms. I lie back and imagine my brain shaken loose by the jackhammering vibrations, the little spiny cells careening in every direction, piling up in sloppy heaps before collecting themselves in swirls inside the circle of my bound, immobilized head. When the noise stops, will I be able to remember the book I started reading yesterday? Will I still be me?

Fifty years ago my parents and I visited Kentucky's Mammoth Cave, descending long switchbacks of stairs into the planet's vast, leaky cavities. Over centuries the milky fish that dart through the cave's subterranean rivers evolved, surviving blind in that darkness. Out here at the surface, though, we aim our instruments—a thousand times more sophisticated than a miner's lamp—into the brain's deep, lightless caverns, and we fret and question, we are frightened by what we can see. *Cavernous hemangioma*: a bloody shadow deep in the brain. Mine could be as old as my time on earth, a capillary constructed incorrectly, leaking blood just this once, no longer mattering: "clinically insignificant." Or it could be a sign of buried danger, observing its own private calendar of disaster.

"Combining multiple MRI sequences," my neurologist tells me, is the only way for us to keep watch for the changes—growth or movement—that reveal the presence of a tumor. We'll not be able to ascertain what's there "with a degree of peace of mind" without returning to the same machine every six months for new images. My doctor flips his computer screen in my direction to show the arrayed slices of brain, touches with the tip of his finger what he wants me to notice. Then he closes the file, leaving only my name spelled out in capital letters at the top of the frame.

*   *   *

It snowed in October this year in New York, thunder cracking over Manhattan, laying waste the unnatural softness, announcing that the order of things is in disarray. My mother and her twin sister are both eighty-six years old, both stiff and short of breath as they face ahead another harsh Chicago winter, the chill threshold of the annual cycle. I cannot shake the thought that I could die before they do. On the subway ride home from the hospital, the bodies crowded around me dissolve into naked brains dancing on stems like Halloween skeletons.

I pass through the city each day wrapped in my invisible difference. Around me the world revolves: the neighbors in the elevator saying good morning as their spaniels and terriers yank on leashes, colleagues with their greetings and their questions, the women grabbing for numbers at the deli smoked fish counter accidentally touching my head without pausing to check for damage or drawing closer to listen for its secrets.

4. GARDEN HUNTER

1

To make a garden you must draw a line. You must run a thread of hope through raw space and pull that thread tight: wall, fence, hedge. As human as the urge to control and to create, to nurture and to separate from wildness, to hold close and to resist incursion. The fragile possibility of perfection, an alternative to the shapeless *now*, the disheveled *here*, the vulnerable *I*.

To start a garden is to wish for difference: *the world as it could be.*

2

I am the daughter of gardeners, and I come to gardens in the long wake of my parents' deaths. In places as familiar as backyards and neighborhood parks, as the conservatories that we visited together, I seek out what allowed my mother and my father to imagine a future forever unfolding, always just a single season away. I come to gardens to be surrounded by growing life, bearing the marks of delight and the scent of what is no longer within my reach. I am a hunter of gardens, of what my parents cherished and clung to.

3

What extravagant expectations American visionaries brought to gardens. John Adams, James Madison, Thomas Jefferson—all of them loaded their letters with recommendations of gardening books and local crop varieties; while Benjamin Franklin's seed exchanges with his correspondents aimed to help the colonies achieve self-sufficiency. After resigning his commission as commander of the Continental Army, George Washington returned to rural Mount Vernon as a gardener, still a slaveholder but committed to working entirely with native American species from across the new country. Magnolias, white pines, live oak, hemlock, and local conifers. When Jefferson dispatched Meriwether Lewis and William Clark in 1804 to explore the lands the U.S. had acquired from France in the Louisiana Purchase, he included instructions to collect local plants that could be established in American gardens.

Two centuries later, John F. Kennedy's shiny idea of a post-World War II American future spun its own garden story. With its winning narration, Jackie Kennedy's Valentine's Day, 1961 television tour of her renovations to the White House created some of the most enduring images of what turned out to be both a fragile and a hopeful time. The White House Rose Garden quickly became one of the most recognizable icons of the vitality and international stature of the U.S. that the Kennedy administration aimed to project. When JFK awarded the seven astronauts of Project Mercury the Collier Trophy in October of 1963, he selected the Rose Garden for the ceremony—and for the photo opportunity with which he burnished the image of his ambitious space program, launching America's "New Frontier."

Members of my parents' generation, many of them first-time suburban homeowners, brought to gardens their own charged hopes for a postwar American Eden. The growth of mail-order giants like Burpee, with their innovative flower and vegetable hybrids, and the rise of the lawn care industry (chemical weed care, home sprinkler systems, and power lawn mowers) fueled that generation's bold assertion of its dominion. My mother and father spent weekends bent over seed catalogs and gardening manuals, analyzing their backyard soil with chemical testing kits that they bought at the neighborhood hardware store and strategizing the plantings of bulbs and seeds that would create their new world from scratch, *tabula rasa*.

4

On my father's bookshelf the Modern Library edition of *Walden*, with its stern torchbearer imprinted on the spine, was a beloved, much-handled thing. Into long winter evenings my father read Thoreau's account of planting beans at Walden Pond—not to eat, for they were not to his taste and Thoreau often exchanged for rice what he'd harvested, but out of love. His bean field linked Thoreau to the freshly handled earth and the sun's force. It set off his imagination and provided a mission to which he could give generously the labor of his heart—and the great gift of reaching my equally solitary father.

To tend to his garden was for Thoreau an act of optimism, an act of faith—yet not at all a remote thing. The fullness of what humans could do on their own—what a human could be—lay in that field within reach of his hands and his hoe, those simple, accessible instruments of radical transformation. To Thoreau and the generations of readers who followed him, the garden offered a close-by site of Creation, of American Genesis; of "making the earth say beans instead of grass."

5

I remember my mother in her gardens. The delicate, light blue bachelor's buttons that she planted with my father. The little house that she bought after my parents' divorce, where a rickety fence sagged between the rows of marigolds that she patiently put in and the ruckus of the supermarket parking lot next door. The raised plot at the retirement home where she could work near the end of her life without stooping. She'd lift a hand as we pushed her wheelchair through the gardens there, calling for a stop so she could name the flowers that she saw: daffodils and tulips; the milkweed that her friends had planted to attract monarch butterflies. "*Damn you, rabbit!*" she cried, waving her arms, when a bunny hopped brazenly from her own plot. And even when she could no longer manage the work of gardening, my mother remained on the lookout for what gardens gave her: "Somebody had a great day putting *those* in," she called out from the back seat of the car where we thought she had dozed off, as we drove past a lush patch of lilies along a busy road.

6

It returns to me from travel, the unique terminology that unlocks this great building, miraculously only blocks from where I live in Manhattan: *transept, nave, choir* and cathedral close, the grounds hugging this beautiful hugeness. I position myself in the garden, where the structure of the cathedral is echoed. Two sharply crossing paths end in pointed archways; recessed corners of topiary mark the perimeters of this set-apart space—*apse?*—in which human hope for the sacred is so deeply felt as to deserve a language of its own.

The stained-glass windows rise over the cloistered rose gardens, extraordinary backdrop, glass and color pushed fragment by fragment to their limits. Set off from the distraction of city streets, the natural world and its cycles are illuminated here, whole: some roses the light-sprinkled pink that signals fresh life, still bending toward the sun; others, their petals browning, already spent.

I hear the wild shrieks of the cathedral peacocks just outside the garden gate—ancient symbols of immortality and renewal, their bodies in mythology resisting decay even after death. I wish one of them would come nearer and parade before me its arrogant transcendence of the ordinary, its long tail feathers studded with green and blue disks—surely too heavy to lift off from the gritty earth.

7

Every garden has a history, time marked in the passing of each season. But more than most, this garden's history is visible. I enter through the high wrought iron gate on Fifth Avenue, its elaborate Beaux Arts style looking back to what one man imagined and another owned.

The way things are laid out here—the lines of benches, the squares of plantings, the climactic fountains and statues—speaks emphatically of design. And for those who wish to know them, the dates and the names are not hard to find: the transplanting in 1939 of the Vanderbilt Gate from old Cornelius's 1883 mansion, forty blocks south; the Conservatory greenhouses built in 1898 and razed in 1934, source of the Garden's name and replaced by six acres of plantings by Depression-era WPA workers; the completed garden's opening to the public in 1937. More than a century of cycles of creation and neglect and revival, of quiet staging of the city's hopes for greatness, its love of pomp and its imposition of order.

Deep inside, the present quiets to a pond closed in by bushes and low trees. Tourists turning the corner lower their voices, respecting the hush. Lily pads spread and float, their lavender blossoms tethered to roots just out of sight. The new season's baby carp set a rhythm, making their way through the water and breaking the pond's skin with their nibbling mouths as they rise and sink.

So many come here like me each day, seeking—refusing to postpone one more moment the chance to witness the raw world polished to a pleasing shape. And yet in a place paced with the seasons, change is always imminent. A siren pushes harsh waves of sound toward the hospital beyond the far hedge. Near to the ghosts of greenhouses, loss hangs thick.

My neighbor on one of the concrete benches surrounding the pond stands up and stretches, then leans to kiss the head of the elderly woman beside her in a wheelchair. "Beautiful mother," she whispers, "I'll be back tomorrow."

8

Children of Japanese American gardeners! In the remote desert at Manzanar and Topaz and Tule Lake they witnessed their mothers and fathers, born in the United States like my own mother and father, planting gardens as soon as they descended from the train cars in the frightened wake of Pearl Harbor. Those children could hardly have known the fullness of what had to be abandoned at the very start of the spring season: the long-tended flower gardens and fruit trees, the vineyards that yielded grapes for homemade wine, the year's farm crops. The recently pruned fruit trees, the acres of seedlings—the work and care and hope of more than one generation. At night they could hear too close by in the dusty camp barracks the lives of others, their coughing and their anger, their weeping loneliness and, sometimes, their love. And in the harsh desert daylight those children witnessed their parents' determination to remain who they had been before: creators, repositories of skill and wisdom; gardeners.

9

In his backyard in soil-smudged Bermuda shorts and a bulging T-shirt, headphones clamped to his head, my father vibrated in the golden late-day light of summer. Like an astronaut loosed in space from the tiresome claims of gravity and the confusing obligations of earthly life, he floated free from the clinging static of family, the uncertainties of his aging body and dimming vision, the encounters with smug younger colleagues. Silky and deep over the track of his labored breaths, Haydn and Bach beamed directly into his ears from WFMT, Chicago's classical station—the same music he pumped into his car on the Sunday afternoons when he drove his sullen, unappreciative teenage daughters into the city to museums and high-end restaurants. Or to his elderly parents' high-rise apartment, where we huddled without knowing what to say to one another at the picture window, Lake Michigan washing soundlessly far below onto the beach.

From his knees all my father could see in his garden, all he could smell, were the pollen-soaked plantings he'd sunk into damp soil with his own hands and sustained with water since the first spring thaw. Distantly, beyond the rim of the concrete patio and the heavy lawn furniture, his wife and his children sat and ate and quarreled, held invisibly at bay.

10

not a sound comes from the empty village
as I stand eating the black cherries
from the loaded branches above me
saying to myself Remember this
(W.S. Merwin, "Black Cherries")

Like witches they flew along rows
Keeping creation at ease;
With a tendril for needle
They sewed up the air with a stem;
They teased out the seed that the cold kept asleep,—
All the coils, loops, and whorls.
They trellised the sun; they plotted for more than themselves.
(Theodore Roethke, "Frau Bauman, Frau Schmidt, and Frau Schwartze")

These beans have results which are not harvested
by me. Do they not grow for woodchucks partly?
The ear of wheat, (in Latin *spica*, obsoletely *speca*,
from *spe*, hope,) should not be the only hope of the
husbandman, its kernel or grain (*granum*, from
gerendo, bearing,) is not all that it bears. How, then,
can our harvest fail?
      (Henry David Thoreau, "The Bean-Field,"
      Walden)

11

My parents, those old gardeners, are both gone now. I am
still their daughter, hoping for clarity at the end—for things to be
made right—but in retrospect the end recedes, farther and farther
out of reach. Time seems instead to circle back and enclose, hiding
what is most tender and needful, leaving exposed only mystery's
resisting outer layer.

12

I know I've let you down, my father kept repeating on his
last phone call to me, low and secretive. *Where are you?* I kept
asking, keeping the conversation going like one of those TV
crime show investigations where the police zeroed in on a caller's
location—drawing silent arcs in the air with their hands, signaling
not to let the conversation end, mouthing the words, *Just a little
longer, we've almost got it,* as radar drew steadily tighter circles on
a map, pinpointing the hidden target.

Later, after I'd hung up, I began putting pieces together,
remembering that my father was seeing a new shrink; suspecting
that my father had suffered a breakdown and been admitted
to a hospital where his memories were now leaking out. The
memories, perhaps, that we never shared with one another: the
Sunday afternoons when he drove drunk in glass-plain daylight,
his wife silent beside him in the front seat of the car, my little sister
and I pressed behind them against opposite windows as he ran
yellow lights and honked at anyone who cut him off, putting all of
us in the wild way of danger. I closed my eyes and let the clues that

my father was dropping, loaded with shame now—*now!*—stack up unacknowledged in my head. Unsolved mystery, floundering man, unhealed hurt.

And the questions that came too late for either of us to answer, laid with him to unsettled rest in the public botanic garden where we cast his ashes on a December day. Beneath the snow, the past year's grass and plantings were frozen. We unpacked the cardboard box and the plastic bag inside and spilled the contents into the harsh morning light of winter.

Even when it's no longer what it was, no longer a solid and animated thing, the body makes its claims upon us: demanding a particular kind of respect, acknowledgment that it once was more than grayish gravel and dust released into cold air too thin to hold it aloft, more than what drifts across the crust of buried, quiescent life.

13

On my mother's last night, I phoned her. One more call like so many others when I expected each of us to work the conversation slowly toward love, to say out loud the words we needed as time, we both knew, was growing short. But that night my mother could not accept the distance of the telephone, the fact that my wife Ellen and I were in New York, together, while she remained in Chicago, alone in her room. *Why is that*, she continued to ask me, *Why are you two there and not here, how did that happen?*

And I trembled, hearing what my mother was saying, something completely different from anything she had ever said. And I asked if she'd like to speak with Ellen, handing over the phone as I spoke, not waiting for her answer. *I don't know what to do!* she whispered to Ellen, and Ellen asked her: *Are you ready for bed yet? No?* I could hear Ellen's calm voice—*Then let the nurse help you get into your nightgown*—and I could hear my mother's faint response: *Okay.* I could see my mother's little room, the bedside table with a couple of paperbacks stacked and her Scrabble dictionary, and the bowls of wrapped snacks—stubby Tootsie Rolls and coffee-flavored candy; granola bars and packets of saltines—replenished from the bags that my sister always bought for her at Walgreen's. I hope that the flowers my sister salvaged from my mother's garden were still fresh on the windowsill, and that my mother let herself lie back, the thinning pink fabric of her old pajamas billowed against the starched white sheet, let herself see one final time what she had made grow. *Good night, I love you,* Ellen said quietly into the phone.

I could not make myself cross the distance to my mother's fear and confusion, but I hope that she did call for a nurse to help her to the bathroom and help her change clothes, to ease her into bed so she could read and rest. And I hope that the room quieted around her, shedding the television noise, the voices she mostly could no longer make out anyway. I hope that my mother wasn't afraid after the nurse left her, by herself in the long night, the street traffic fading away below her window. I surely hope that the time—*what was she asking me?*—was right.

5. FOR RICHARD (EVERY LOVE ITS OWN WORLD)

You tried to color my hair at the kitchen sink the night we moved in together: a big man wielding a little brush with surprising delicacy, applying blond dye in practiced streaks. Too much, too soon—I washed it out after ten minutes over your laughing protests. In the night I tiptoed past your bed to our single bathroom, pausing for cold, barefoot minutes at two men's naked bodies tangled in sheets.

We roamed the beautiful world together, letting magic wash over us. We crossed the Alps in your straining Fiat, snapping one another's pictures by the side of the road as we entered the legendary passes, the clouds drifting so low they left their cold touch on our shoulders. Growing up in the flat Midwest, I'd never driven so close to the sky. At a ruined Loire Valley chateau at dusk, a peacock dropped from a tree—impossibly near!—and spread its jeweled feathers. We hiked at twilight into a long ravine on a Navajo reservation where dwellings of the Anasazi were scored into rock, hoarding their story of lost life. On the canyon floor a small pasture remained, green against the sheer, rust-streaked walls. A young shepherd rang a bell just once, as his ancestors must have done for generations, and his flock of sheep followed him into the faltering light.

We fed in secret together on junk we foraged at the Seven-Eleven, Hostess Ding-Dongs and Suzy-Q's that we stowed in the freezer and then lingered over, licking out the cold layers of frosting, letting the cheap chocolate cake melt against our cheeks' warm tenderness, laughing, until what we were eating was hardly food, what we were doing was hardly eating, what we were feeling was wild: wild, raw hunger.

And we came to share the dark knowledge of the chronically ill. The impossibility of counting on our bodies, the unwelcome sensation of chemicals beating deep in our blood; the newly revealed terms of survival, and their limits. We both hated the lingering taste—like a spreading internal film—of bad hospital food, hated the too-small gowns, the gritty feel of unwashed hair and incomplete showers. You wept when you told me you'd heard a nurse refer to you in the hall as "that old man."

At Jaime's last Christmas dinner, before AIDS finally took

him, you and I laid out turkey and chestnut stuffing, fennel salad with bright orange slices. But he pushed away his plate, pushed his chair away from the table. We could hear the spaniel puppy Jaime had recently bought, scratching and whining alone in a wire enclosure in the back yard, and we both knew it was wrong, this acquisition of a creature that the closeness of death had already made it impossible for him to care for. But we remained silent, witnesses to his as yet undiminished appetite for hope.

"I wish for more life for both of us and I wish it keenly," you wrote to me after my initial diagnosis. But I have outlived you, my friend.

At your memorial service I heard so many remember you as their brother, so many whom I didn't know, whom I never heard you speak of. Who are all these men who call you beloved? I am surprised, now that you are gone, by how much you held back from me.

You confided to me many times how your mother claimed all the grief for herself after your father died, when you were only ten. And I wondered at your mother's love for you, and your love for your mother; at the charged and tender place between need and generosity.

Perhaps every love is its own world.

On our return drive toward the Alps, a fog descended without warning on the *autostrada*. We were flying through cold, impenetrable mist, the hood of our car impossible to see, the side of the road where we might pull over invisible. Our speeding capsule filled with your cigarette smoke, matching the cloud into which we were blindly dissolved and the hot-breathed fear that belongs to genuine danger. I laid my hand over yours, over the hand that was gripped anxiously to the steering wheel. And the world shrank to this hurtling thing, fragile metal and flesh, letting whiteness enclose us, only us.

6. IN THE PHOTIC ZONE

The perimeters of my early years: a half-dozen streets unfolding in three directions and then the fourth, work of the final glaciers, Lake Michigan and its beaches. In summer I floated on the great water, shiver-cold until September, stretched nearly to the Canadian border where it reaches its most deep—deeper than life, below the photic zone that marks the limits of photosynthesis. When I emerged on my knees, the lake releasing my body from the shallows, I could see hundreds of towels and umbrellas opened across the beach to the warming sun.

Breaking the sand's crust with our shovels, my sister and I easily reached the water table, carving moats around our castles or moistening the drying walls before they crumbled. At some point during the afternoon, we would join the restless wait for ice cream. Our mother knew from the changing angle of the sun exactly when it was time to shake off the clinging sand and get dressed again for the short walk home. After dinner, when the summer light stretched on, we might head back into the streets on our bikes with friends, ringing the bells at the ends of our handlebars, circling our territory over and over. Soon we would hear our parents' voices reach out for us, and we would turn back.

Astronauts recognize from outer space the far-away home planet to which they will return, speeding at three thousand degrees Fahrenheit through the resisting atmosphere and parachuting back into remote ocean waters. In the photos they take from orbit, the coastline of Lake Michigan and its seasons are clear: hooded in white by ice and snow in winter, ringed in green by algae in late summer.

Wild things, too, lock into orbit: feel the planet as an irresistible, electromagnetic force, drawing them back to the same places year after year, the places where each generation creates the generation that follows. The sky—the shifting light of the sun and the moon; the positions of the stars—provides a compass that sea turtles and crabs, dung beetles and indigo buntings all follow home. Pole to pole, terns circle the planet, scraping the bare earth to nest and breed in open places near water, then migrating to Antarctica where they spend the Southern Hemisphere summer, a round-trip flight of more than twenty-five thousand miles.

Today a single gull beats the air above the shore, skims the water's surface, then rises against the pastel sky. Suddenly Canada geese appear overhead, honking, moving in to scout for food. I can feel the sound they make echoing in my own body, so aware am I in this my seventieth year not only of the markers of the changing seasons but, equally, of my own season turning. Few living things signal the cyclical shape of life in a more stately way than geese in V formation in the high sky, their wings spread wide, coasting, working the air.

Yet these birds are not headed further south, I know. They no longer follow the ancient flyways to winter along the warm Atlantic coast, as distant as Miami. Here in the city, where predator populations have declined, they've learned to forage in the grass and the garbage of public parks and to find warm spots to sleep on rooftops of houses and factory buildings, conserving energy to shorten their return flight north in spring. Their droppings splatter in parks and they waddle on land, awkward big birds like any others.

The beach is diminished now as well, eroded by the lake's steady rise over the past decade, and my mother has been gone for nearly five years. Many miles north along the shoreline, the water has engulfed entire houses, unexpectedly buried what humans built and lived in. And even here, where what's left remains sufficient to accommodate running dogs and a lifeguard stand and several rows of beach umbrellas, the crescent of sand narrowing toward a wall of raw boulders feels like loss. No one knows if the lake is just making gentle adjustments or if it is returning to prehistoric levels—if it could once again cover the surrounding land.

Who am I now, returning to this place, turning toward the end of my own short history? I am a creature in thrall like so many others to the forces that turn this planet: a creature tuned to magnetism and to cycles. I walk the sand's damp edge where my mother and my aunt brought my sister and my cousins and me half a century ago, undressing their still-young bodies and the bodies of their children, spreading beach towels and unpacking picnic lunches, unafraid of the sun.

With Thanks

My work over the ten years of writing these essays has been
shaped and supported by two especially precious readers, and I'm
so glad for the chance to thank both of them here:
David Sugarman, for his wisdom and large-heartedness as a
reader and a friend;
and Ellen Wertheim—every word, every day.

After nearly fifty years in Vermont and New York City, **Joanne Jacobson** has returned to the Midwest where she grew up—and to writing about home. Her most recent book, *Every Last Breath: A Memoir of Two Illnesses*, came out in 2020 from The University of Utah Press. She has also published an earlier memoir, *Hunger Artist: A Suburban Childhood* (2007), and a monograph, *Authority and Alliance in the Letters of Henry Adams* (1992).

Her writing has appeared in such publications as *New England Review, Fourth Genre, BOMB, Florida Review, Bellevue Literary Review, Southwest Review,* and *The Nation,* and has been cited in *Best American Essays* and nominated for a Pushcart Prize. She is retired from Yeshiva University, where she taught courses on nonfiction writing and on American literature and culture.

For more about Joanne Jacobson and her work:
https://www.joannejacobson.com/